AMAZING SPORTS

BASKETBALL

BY LORI DITTMER

CREATIVE EDUCATION • CREATIVE PAPERBACKS

Published by Creative Education and Creative Paperbacks
P.O. Box 227, Mankato, Minnesota 56002
Creative Education and Creative Paperbacks are imprints of
The Creative Company
www.thecreativecompany.us

Design by The Design Lab
Production by Dana Koehler
Art direction by Rita Marshall
Printed in the United States of America

Photographs by Alamy (FL Historical 1A, Andrew Fredrickson/Southcreek Global/ZUMApress.com, Paola Visone/Pacific Press), Dreamstime (Richard Kane, Torsak), iStockphoto (AlexanderZam, IPGGutenbergUKLtd, pisagor, Renphoto), Newscom (Mingo Nesmith/Icon Sportswire DIL/M. Anthony Nesmith/Icon Sportswire), Shutterstock (Aspen Photo, KoQ Creative, Pukhov K, Red Confidential)

Library of Congress Cataloging-in-Publication Data
Names: Dittmer, Lori, author.
Title: Basketball / Lori Dittmer.
Series: Amazing sports.
Includes index.
Summary: Get the ball rolling with this high-interest introduction to basketball, the sport known for its hoops and orange balls. Also included is a biographical story about professional basketball player and coach Becky Hammon.

Identifiers:
ISBN 978-1-64026-212-6 (hardcover)
ISBN 978-1-62832-775-5 (pbk)
ISBN 978-1-64000-347-7 (eBook)
This title has been submitted for CIP processing under LCCN 2019937922.

First Edition HC 9 8 7 6 5 4 3 2 1
First Edition PBK 9 8 7 6 5 4 3 2 1

Table of Contents

Basketball Beginnings	4
Equipment	7
The Game	11
Player Positions	15
Amazing Basketball	19
Story of a Player: Becky Hammon	22
Read More	24
Websites	24
Index	24

In 1891, James Naismith came up with a new game. Players tried to shoot a soccer ball into a peach basket at the end of a court. Each time the ball went in, someone had to get it back out! The baskets were soon replaced by hoops.

James Naismith became the first basketball coach at the University of Kansas in 1898.

Backboards are usually made of special glass that is hard to break.

Today, hoops are mounted 10 feet (3 m) high on walls or posts. Behind the hoop is a rectangular backboard. The only other piece of equipment is the ball. National Basketball Association (NBA) basketballs are 29.5 inches (74.9 cm) around. Youth **leagues** use smaller balls.

leagues groups of sports clubs that play each other over a period of time for a championship

People can play basketball outside or inside. Different parts of the court have special names. The game starts in the center jump circle. Baselines are behind each basket. The three-second area is called the "paint."

On most courts, the painted part below the free throw line is where the "paint" is.

MARILYN
STEPHENS
33
JOHN
CHANEY
CLASS
OF
2001
WOMEN'S
BASKETBALL
RUTGERS
0
RUTGERS
15
TEMPLE
3
$171
Million
24

A basketball game is broken into four quarters. Two teams play against each other. Each team has five players on the court. The team trying to score is called the offense.

The other team plays defense, trying to stop the offense's shots.

Players are always watching to see who might be open to receive a pass.

To move the ball, a player must **dribble** or pass it. The defense may block or **steal** the ball. Most baskets are worth two points. The team with the most points at the end of the game wins.

dribble to move the ball forward by continuously bouncing it with one hand while walking or running

steal a forced turnover

A coach's job is to help lead her players—during a game and elsewhere.

The coach is in charge of the team. Each person on the court has a job. The center plays near the hoop. This person blocks shots and grabs **rebounds**. The small forward is good at passing and shooting.

rebounds balls that bounce back after hitting the backboard

Power forwards catch passes to shoot near the basket. The shooting guard can make shots from all over the court. The point guard leads the team and keeps the ball moving.

Point guard Trey Burke played college ball at Michigan before turning pro.

MICHIGAN
3
Penn State
Alumni A ation

USA

Center Brittney Griner has played for the U.S. in the Olympics and other events.

People of all ages play basketball. In the United States, the NBA and Women's National Basketball Association (WNBA) are for professional athletes. Basketball has been a part of the Summer **Olympic Games** since 1936.

Olympic Games a set of international sports competitions which take place every four years

Basketball is popular around the world. It is easy to learn. The rules have not changed much over time. Shoot some hoops with friends, and enjoy this amazing game!

Naismith's original 13 rules are still part of today's game of basketball.

Story of a Player: Becky Hammon

Becky Hammon grew up in South Dakota. She started playing basketball as a toddler. She played every day with her older brother and her dad. In high school, Becky was a star player. She graduated from Colorado State University as the school's all-time scoring leader. In 1999, she joined the WNBA's New York Liberty. Later, she played for the San Antonio Stars. She earned the nickname "Big Shot Becky" for her ability to score under pressure. Becky retired from professional play in 2014. Then she became an assistant coach for the San Antonio Spurs. She is one of the first women to join an NBA coaching staff.

adidas

Read More

Bodden, Valerie. *Basketball.* Mankato, Minn.: Creative Education, 2016.

Ervin, Phil. *12 Reasons to Love Basketball.* North Mankato, Minn.: Bookstaves, 2018.

Websites

DK Find Out: Basketball
https://www.dkfindout.com/us/sports/basketball/
Learn how to move the ball down the court in basketball.

Ducksters: Sports – Basketball
https://www.ducksters.com/sports/basketball.php
Read about basketball history, including some famous pro players.

Note: Every effort has been made to ensure that the websites listed above are suitable for children, that they have educational value, and that they contain no inappropriate material. However, because of the nature of the Internet, it is impossible to guarantee that these sites will remain active indefinitely or that their contents will not be altered.

Index

balls 7, 12, 16
coaches 15, 22
courts 8, 11, 15, 16
Hammon, Becky 22
hoops 4, 7
leagues 7, 19, 22
Naismith, James 4
Olympic Games 19
players 11, 12, 15, 16, 19, 22
scoring 11, 12, 22